What people are saying about …

COTTONMOUTH AND THE RIVER

"Casey Fritz has given families a deep and profound truth in a childlike way. With beautiful illustrations and heart-changing words, *Cottonmouth and the River* is a must-add to every young parent's library. My heart was moved by the story, and my guess is yours will be too."

Elyse Fitzpatrick, author of *Give Them Grace*

"It is rare to find a book in this genre as wonderfully written and beautifully drawn as *Cottonmouth and the River*. Even more rare is to find them packed with the themes of sacrifice and redemption. This book is a gift."

Tim Chaddick, father of three, founding pastor at Reality LA, and author of *Better*

"'Read it again!' We've read many books as a family, but I can't remember the last time we read one that left my kids saying those words. This one did. It's not often that a story takes our family through emotionally unexpected turns, or that my eight-year-old grabs my arm in nervous anticipation of what's going to happen next. Vivid imagination is unleashed in these pages, and it leaves even young minds suspicious that the story is pointing to a greater one. Engaging art such as this is a foretaste of the kingdom of God."

Al Abdulla, father of three and
pastor at Reality Boston

"In the wilderness of Christian children's books, many mirages exist promising an oasis but instead offer the dry sands of moralism. Casey's book stands like that famous Rock in the desert, offering the thirsty and weary the cool, sweet waters of the gospel. I, with fresh tears in my eyes, recommend this book not only to kids but to adults as well, that we might all be reminded by this wonderful, beautifully drawn story of the great adventurous story we are all in."

Josh Kehler, father of four and
pastor at Reality Stockton

"Artistic, poetic, mysterious, and ingenious, *Cottonmouth and the River* is a great read. It digs its hooks into you and pulls you deep into the story's world. After I finished reading it to my kids, the first thing they said was, 'Can we read it again, Dad?'"

John Mark Comer, father of three
and pastor at A Jesus Church

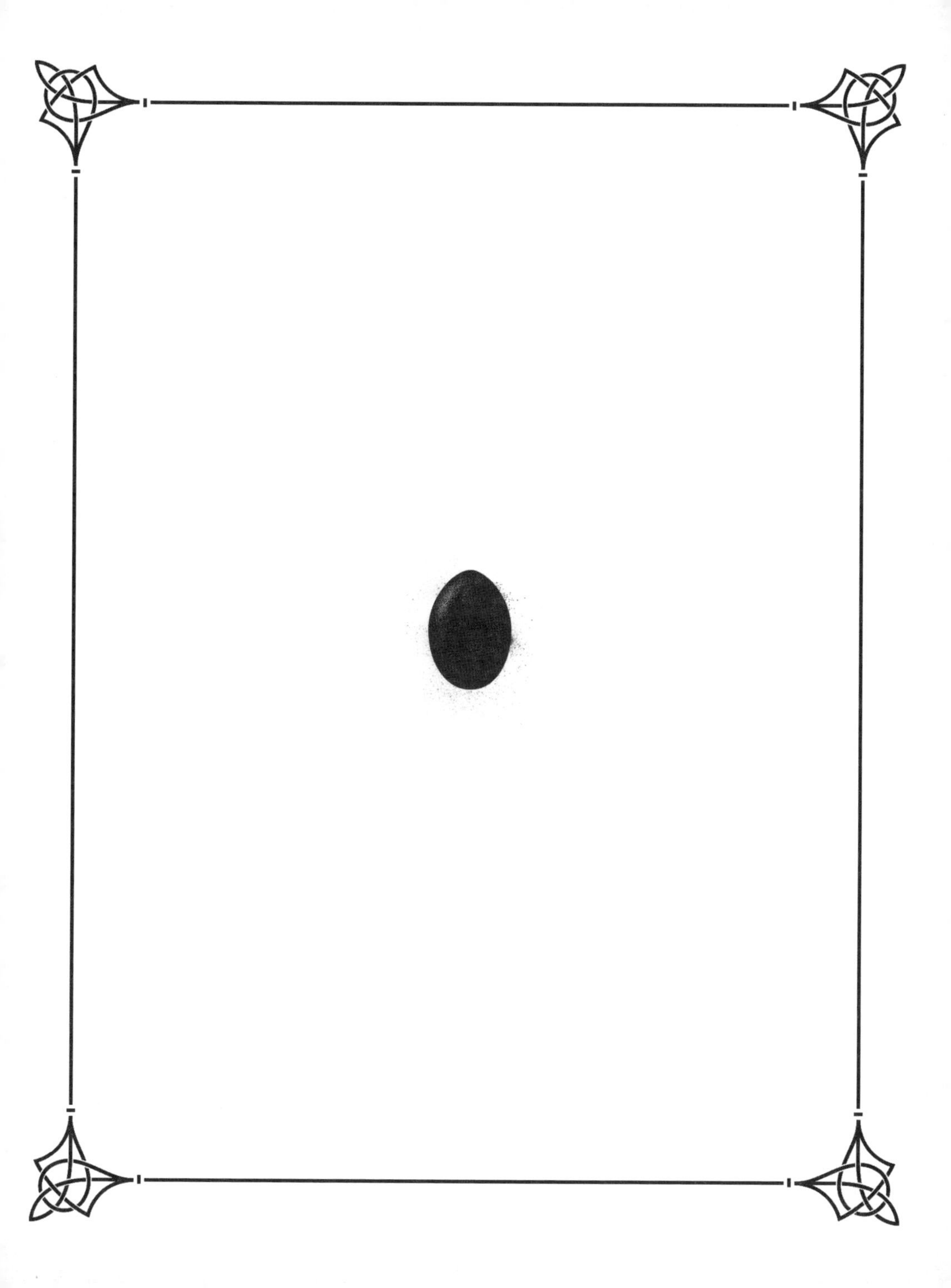

COTTONMOUTH AND THE RIVER
Published by David C Cook
4050 Lee Vance View
Colorado Springs, CO 80918 U.S.A.

David C Cook Distribution Canada
55 Woodslee Avenue, Paris, Ontario, Canada N3L 3E5

David C Cook U.K., Kingsway Communications
Eastbourne, East Sussex BN23 6NT, England

The graphic circle C logo is a registered trademark of David C Cook.

This story is a work of fiction. Characters and events are the product of the author's imagination. Any resemblance to any person, living or dead, is coincidental.

LCCN 2013955268
ISBN 978-0-7814-1033-5
eISBN 978-1-4347-0749-9

Published in association with literary agency D. C. Jacobson & Associates LLC, an Author Management Company. www.dcjacobson.com

The Team: Alex Field, Amy Konyndyk, Tonya Osterhouse, Karen Athen
Cover Design: C. S. Fritz and Phil Schorr
Cover Illustration: C. S. Fritz

Printed in the United States of America
First Edition 2014

1 2 3 4 5 6 7 8 9 10

022614

David C Cook®

For Moses—may you never stop creating monsters
and imagining the impossible.

Also, a very special thanks to Phil Schorr and Bob Smiley,
whose creative contributions to this book truly
make it as special as it is.

COTTONMOUTH

Every day for the past two years, Frederick Cottonmouth had walked to the churning white river near his little home. It was here that Frederick chewed on long blades of grass and tried to hook Apache trout. Only once had a fish ever bitten the end of his crooked, baitless pole.

And every day for the past two years, the river had been a friend to Frederick. Never once had it cut off Frederick while he told a funny story or given him a disapproving look when he became angry. In truth, what made the river so easy to get along with was the fact that it never really tried to communicate with Frederick at all.

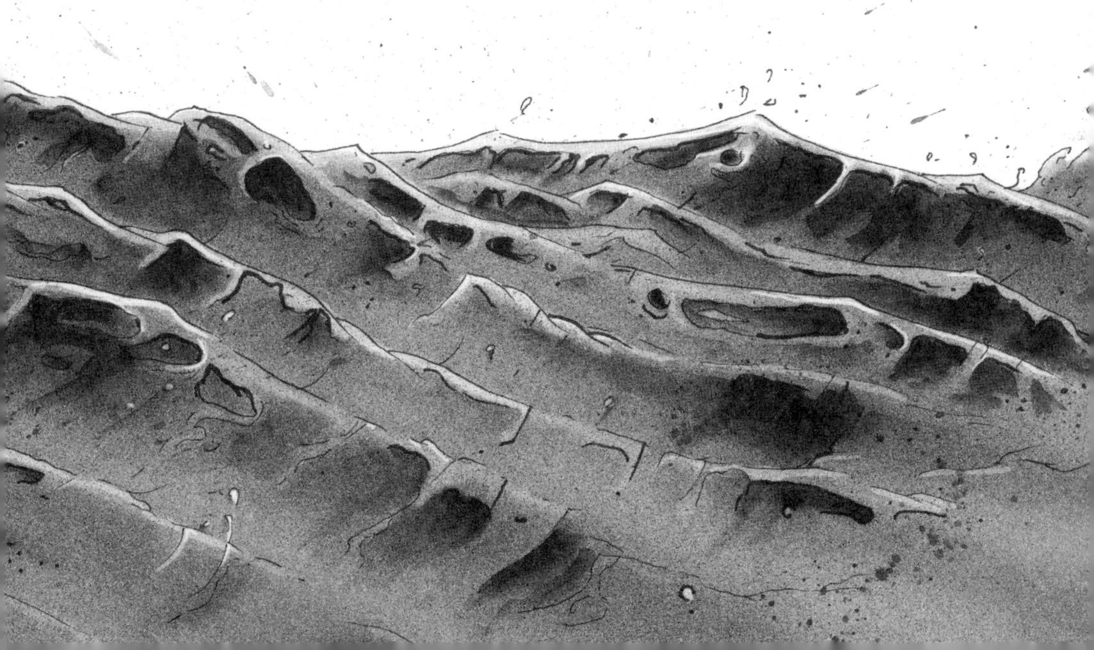

All of That changed One DAY

As he stepped from his house, everything seemed normal. The grasshoppers were hopping. The clouds were in the same place they always were. The yellow leaves … yellow.

But on this particular day, as Frederick approached the river, the water was still. No Apache trout, no movement, no flow. He'd always had to imagine what the stones beneath the rushing water looked like, but today they sat naked and visible, staring up at him like dozens of giant round eyes.

And Frederick, sensing a challenge, stared back.

Now only the stubbornest of boys could think of winning such a contest, but that was Frederick. He stared till his eyes were cold. Till they were dry. Till they felt like chipping paint on an old fence. And then, to his amazement, the stones blinked.

Their winking was the result of a lone ripple passing along the surface of the water. With his eyes, Frederick retraced the ripple's path up the river until he found its cause.

A distant object slowly floated along. It was black—the darkest black little Freddie had ever seen. The shape was harder to tell from such a distance—round but not too round, like the shape of … an egg?

Frederick had spent enough time at the river's edge to have seen a number of strange things float by.

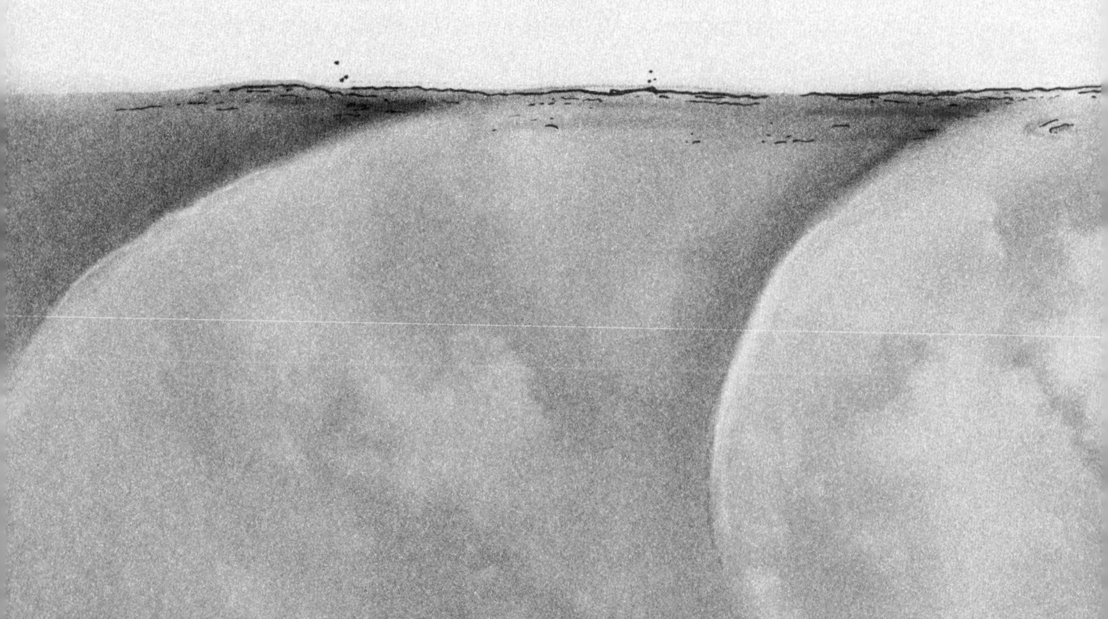

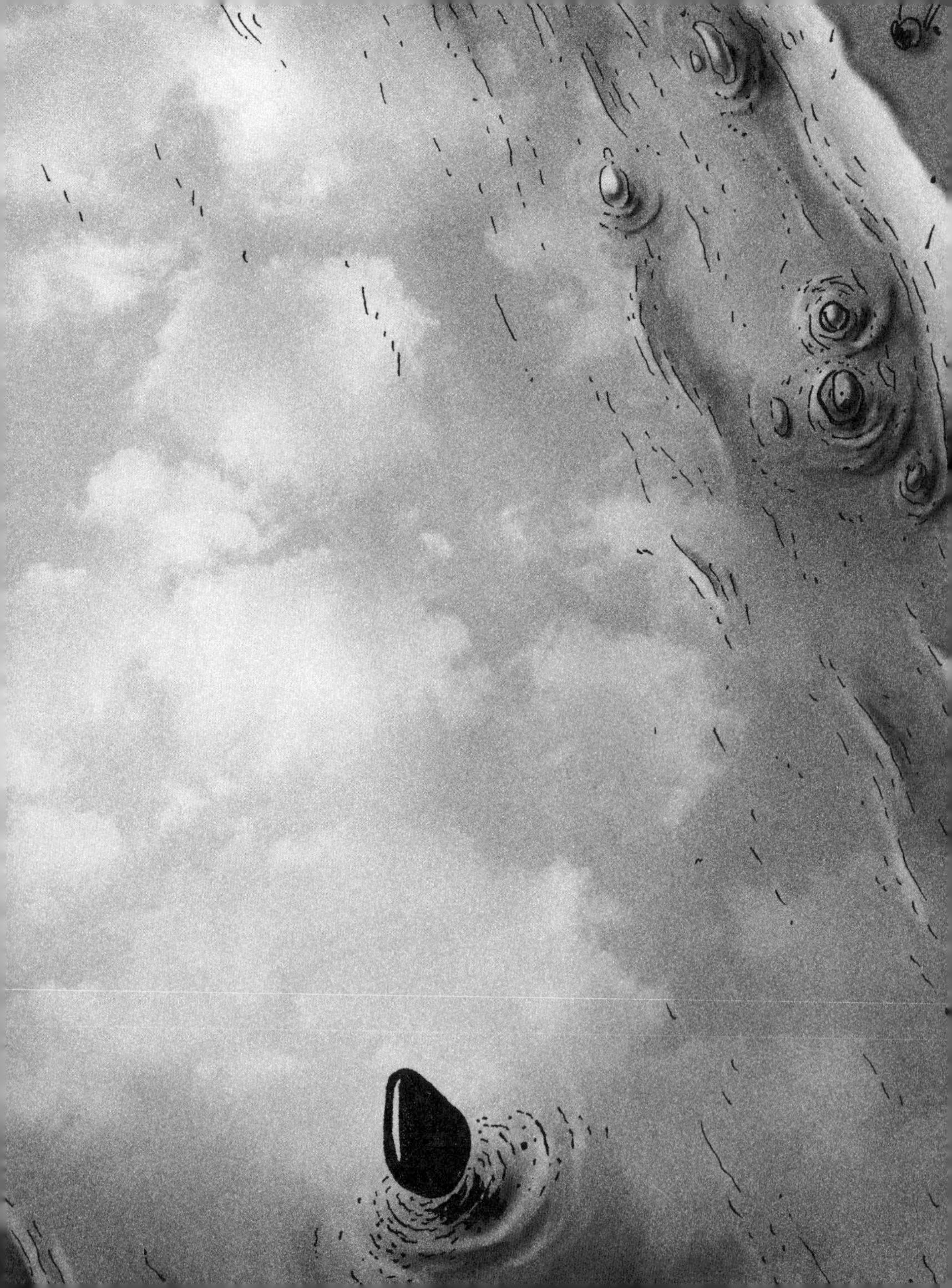

Of course, this egg wasn't floating by.

In a straight line, it came toward Frederick, as if all it wanted was to be close to him—like he'd always dreamed a trout would behave if he were ever to reel one in. Freddie stood as motionless as the river.

It came to the edge of the river and stopped at his feet. Frederick froze, confused by the river's black egg.

Frederick poked the egg with the cork handle of his fishing pole. It sank for a moment, then popped back up. He looked up and down the riverbank to see if anyone would claim it, then finally, he knelt down and picked it up.

The moment he pulled the egg from the water, the river began rushing with life again.

Frederick put the egg in the glass jar he normally used for catching fireflies and ran home. He was chased by a heavy rain, and by the time he reached the back door, Freddie was drenched.

The Cottonmouths had lived in the same house since Frederick was born. He knew every shadow on its walls and every creak in its aging wood floors, from the quick mouselike creaks of the kitchen to the long and slow ones near the top of the staircase. What he didn't know was that this would be his last night in this house for quite some time.

For the black egg, as Frederick suspected, was not a normal egg.

In fact, it really wasn't an egg at all.

It was more of a wish.

An opportunity.

A catapult between dreams and reality.

As the rain beat against the roof of the Cottonmouth residence, night fell quickly, and Frederick settled on the floor of the living room, using his father's old red lantern for both light and warmth. He turned the egg over and over in his hands, wondering and wanting.

He scanned the surface of the shell a few dozen times, looking for clues. It was a flawless egg, with not even a knick or a scratch. He shook it, but there was no response from inside. He even tried to *open* it, starting with a gentle tap with the handle of the lantern and building to an all-out pound. This was an indestructible egg.

He couldn't explain it, but deep in his heart, Frederick knew this was the solution to his sadness. This was something special.

And in turn, *he* was special.

Frederick was almost asleep when he heard a loud *CRACK* upstairs. Then a *BOOM*! Frederick dropped the egg, raced to the bottom of the stairs, and looked up into the darkness of the second floor.

He hadn't gone upstairs for two years.

He had only ever gone as far as the first step, and that was one step farther than he was willing to go now. He grabbed the closest thing to him to use as a weapon … a lit candle.

Another CRACK

He cried out to the intruder, "I HAVE A SWORD!" and raised his arm, ready to throw the candle in his or her … or *its* face.

Just like the river had been earlier, the house went silent.

Frederick looked down, feeling his heart beat fast beneath his wet shirt.

He also saw the egg. Moving. It rolled over to the lantern, slowly. Then it started to spin in a counterclockwise motion. Faster and faster until …

BOOM! Then a mighty *ROOOOOAARRR*!

It was overwhelming! Deep and booming. *What was it?* Frederick thought. It sounded like a … a … laugh.

Whatever was up there was *laughing* at Frederick.

"A sword?" the intruder questioned.

"Yes, a sword! Who are you? What do you want?!" Frederick cried in a throaty shout, trying to sound like his father and not the ten-year-old he was.

“I’m exactly what you wanted,” it said. “I have come to remove your confusion and tell you about your new possession. May I come down and introduce myself, Frederick? Please?” it asked.

Frederick stood there, his shock mixing with confusion. The intruder didn’t wait for him to say yes. The footsteps of whatever this hefty thing was creaked—one long, slow creak—and stopped in the dark at the top of the stairs.

Freddie stood ready to attack. Ready to yell. Ready to do something!

Until he saw it.

The creature.

Each step the beast took down the stairs made Frederick gasp for air.

Before he knew it, it stood right in front of him. Its large belly nearly knocked Frederick over. The candle Frederick held cast light on its long brown fur. Patches of umber and yellow splashed in no particular pattern across its chest, as if it had recently been wrestling a bucket of yellow paint. Its round eyes matched its spots.

Its spiraled horns reminded Frederick of the Barhead rams that grazed by the river.

Little Freddie couldn't even take in all of it before it stuck its overgrown hand in the boy's face and, with a burst of overjoyed energy, let out,

I'M TUG the COMFORTER

Frederick, entertaining his assumed dream, plopped his hand in Tug's hand and replied, "I'm Frederick the Reckless. Or at least that's what my mother used to call me."

"Well, Frederick the Reckless, I regret to inform you that your 'sword' is actually a wax candle."

By this time, the egg had stopped spinning. It was lying perfectly still.

"Ah, there it is," Tug said as he grinned with anticipation.

"What? How do you know about that?" Frederick replied.

"Well, that's why I'm here, Frederick: to reveal to you the amazing possibilities you have within your grasp! You asked the egg—as you call it—for an explanation, and it answered!"

Frederick walked over to pick up the egg.

"Whatever you could possibly want to do, whatever you could possibly imagine … the egg will provide."

Frederick held the egg gently. "I don't understand, Tug," he said quietly.

“Frederick, the river knows your pain. The river feels your sorrow. It has decided to bless you by giving you new life. It wants you to have joy,” Tug said, gingerly taking the egg in his shovel-sized hand. “It wants you to live a life not in waiting but in *doing*!”

Frederick hesitated to accept this, and Tug seemed to know why.

“Do you understand that the river loves you, Frederick?”

Freddie shook his head. “How does the river know this? How does the river know any of this?” Freddie asked as his eyes crept to an old wood frame hanging near the window.

“It knows Freddie. It was there,” Tug replied.

Freddie whipped his head left and right, not wanting Tug to see his tears rolling down his cheeks.

"So I can do anything?" Freddie asked.

"Yes, but there is one thing you can't do. You must promise never to eat the egg," Tug replied.

"Eat it?!" Freddie said, disgusted.

"Never eat it. Promise me!" Tug said loudly, looking deep into Frederick's eyes.

"Sheesh, I promise," Frederick replied, and crossed his heart somewhat sarcastically. There was no way Freddie would ever eat the egg. Frederick *hated* normal eggs—much less black, spinning ones.

"Well, good then! What adventure do you want to embark on first?" Tug said as he tossed the egg back to Freddie.

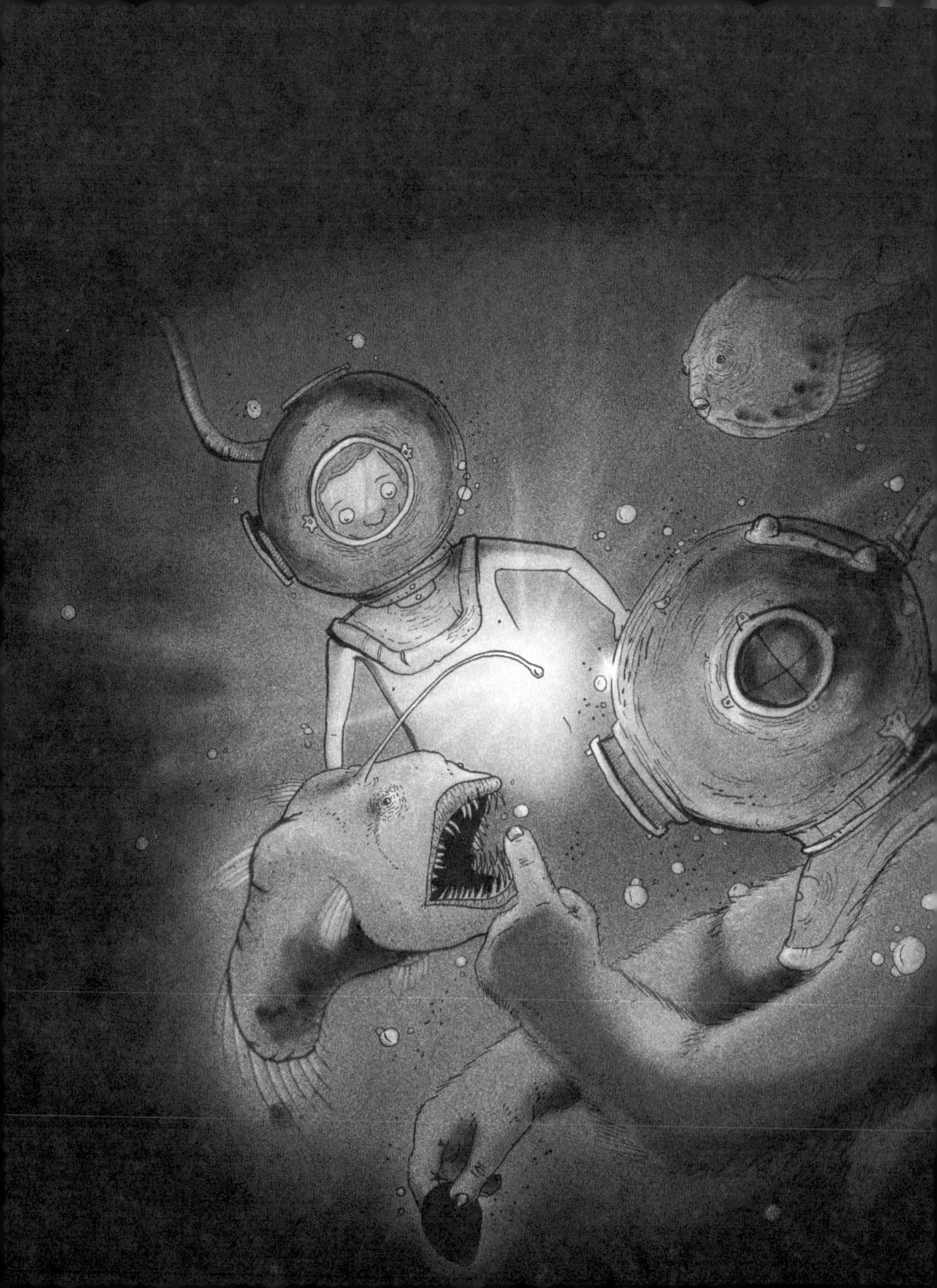

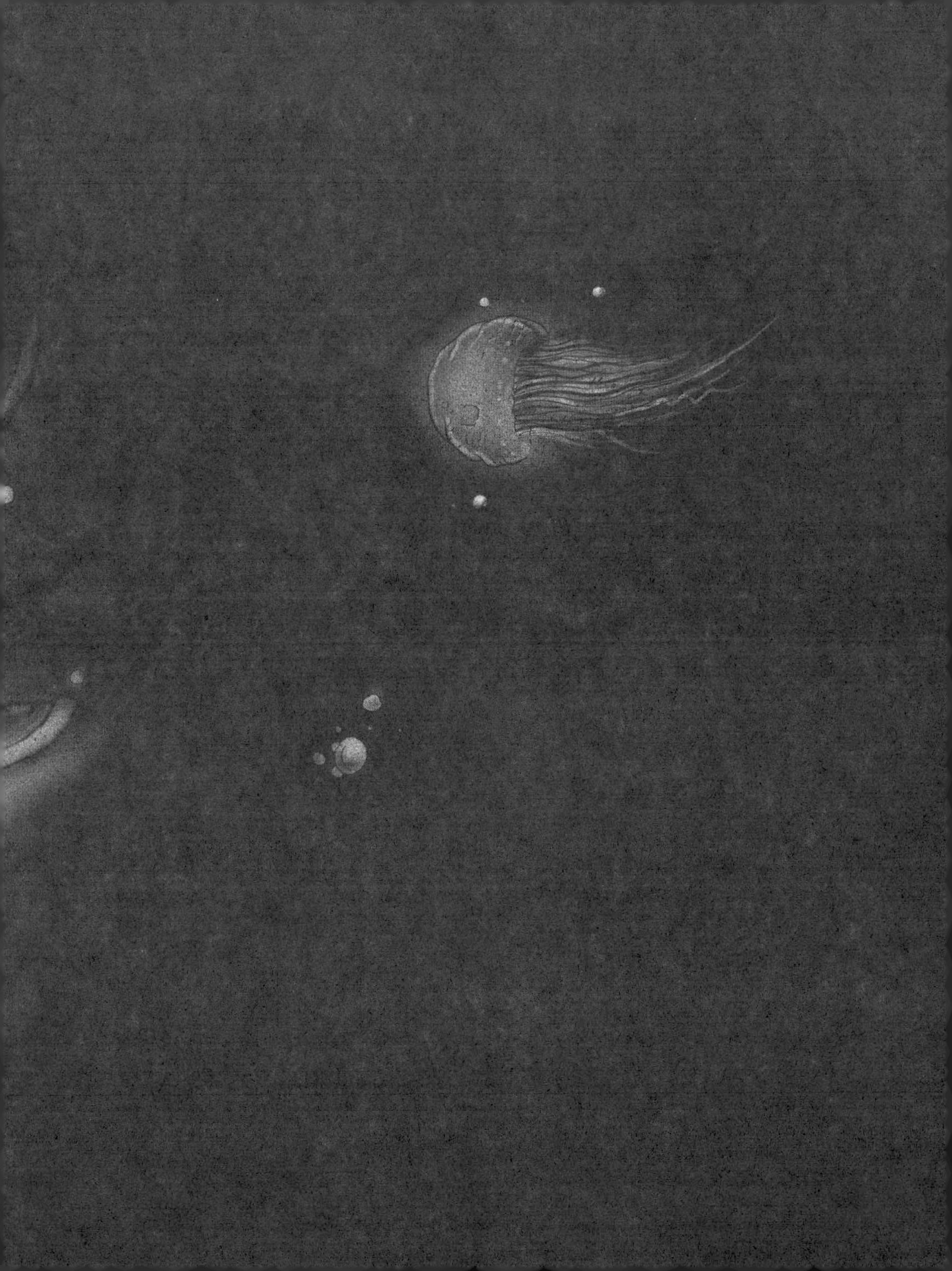

It was an amazing and eventful two weeks. Frederick went on adventures children only dream of!

The last time Frederick was this happy, he had been with his parents. Frederick missed them very much and wanted them back. In fact, he had been waiting for just the right moment to ask Tug about them.

"Tug, I have been thinking a lot. About what I want, about what makes me the happiest. And I wanted to know if the river's black egg would give my parents back," Frederick asked.

Tug stopped and closed his book. He wrapped his arm around Frederick.

"Freddie, have you ever heard the tale of the Sun brothers?"

Frederick shook his head no.

"The story goes that two Suns were born at the exact same moment in time. One was bright and warm to rule the day, and the other cold and gray to rule the night. The dark Sun was always sad and envious of the bright Sun. Everyone loved the bright Sun. They would come out and play with him whenever he shone. But the dark Sun, all would abandon and forget he was there. Well, one day, the angry gray Sun didn't come out at night. He hid from the world and all the people."

"The world was empty of light, and blackness filled the land. People began crying and shouting for the dark Sun to return. You see, Freddie, it was then that the Moon realized that even though he didn't get what he wanted, he was exactly what he needed to be. This similar truth is for you now."

Freddie stood and began to walk back toward the castle, where his old home had once stood, leaving Tug behind.

Tug cried out, "Freddie! Please stay! I need you to trust me."

Frederick was upset and confused as to why he could have *everything* … but not what he wanted most of all. This time he let the tears fall down his cheeks, and he took the egg from his pocket.

Halfway between the river and his home, he stopped to look down at it with disdain.

He then threw the egg as far as his ten-year-old arm could throw it. "If I can't have what I want, I don't want anything at all!" Frederick yelled as the egg raced through the air.

He ran the rest of the way home and slammed the door behind him. After a few seconds, there was a knock.

And then a second.

And then a third.

Frederick stopped and turned back. They were the three quietest knocks Frederick had ever heard. "Tug?"

Knock …

"Tug, I don't want to be bothered," he said with a sigh.

Another knock … this time so quiet it couldn't even be called a knock; it was more of a tap.

Frederick opened the door quickly. "Not now, Tug!"

The threshold was empty.

Or was it?

Excuse me, but I believe this belongs to you

Frederick looked down to see a white rat staring up at him. He was cleaning gold-rimmed glasses and sitting on the black egg Frederick had tossed away just moments before.

"This is yours, isn't it?" the rat asked again.

"How are you talking?" Freddie asked.

"Please, Frederick. You have spent the last two weeks with a dumpy behemoth. A nearsighted talking rat is the least of your worries. I come from the same place your fat friend Tug hails from. I'm here because you want me here."

"I do?" asked Frederick.

"You do," said the rodent. "My name is Menson, and I am here to give you everything you ever wanted."

"I've heard that before," Frederick replied.

"Frederick, let me explain. There are a few things that disgust me. One, cheese. Just because I come from a long line of *rattus* doesn't mean I like it. Two, when people discuss their previous night's dreams. And three, I do not like to be perceived as a liar. Do you want your parents back or not?"

All Frederick could do was stare in shock.

"Then take the black egg and swallow it," Menson said as he climbed off of it.

"What? I can't! I promised Tug I wouldn't," Frederick replied.

"What did that overweight stuffed animal tell you? He said, 'Don't eat it.' Whereas *I* am telling you to take the entire egg and *swallow* it. Eating involves chewing and digestion. Swallowing, on the other hand, allows the egg to pass safely through your body, granting you your heart's innermost desire: your parents' return."

Frederick was torn.

"It's now or never, Frederick. This offer only stands once. If you don't want it, I will be on my merry way." Menson rolled the egg closer to Frederick's feet. "Swallow it, and have everything you have ever wanted."

Frederick looked toward the river for any sight of Tug. He didn't know why, but he felt that if he could just see Tug, he'd know what to do. *Where are you?* Frederick thought.

But Frederick was alone.

Menson began to hum as he waited for Frederick's decision. It was an unusual hum. It had no melody, no joy, no tune.

Without another thought, Frederick reached down, picked up the egg, tilted his head back, and swallowed it.

All went silent, and then the humming started again.

What have I done? Frederick thought.

Menson turned around and began to walk away.

"Wait! Where are you going? Where are my parents?" Frederick cried out to the rat.

"I am done here, Frederick," he said. "My job was to see if you would heed the words of Tug or if your desires were greater than the river's. I'm sorry, but the egg passing through your body will make you very, very sick. I suggest you find shelter and prepare for a lot of hardship. Until next time, Frederick!" Menson disappeared into the field.

Frederick stood there thinking about Tug, thinking about the river, thinking about what he had given up to find his parents.

He had been eight years old when his parents had taken him to the big river by their little home. They'd given Frederick a sack of sandwiches, a jar of water, and a hug. Their instructions were clear: "Frederick Cottonmouth, we will meet you here later, at this exact spot." And then they walked off, never to return. And every day for the past two years, Frederick waited by the river for them with as much hope as a young boy could muster.

As Frederick walked back into the huge mansion, he indeed felt very weak. His stomach began to writhe with pain.

He rested against the wall in the kitchen, not noticing at first that the castle was starting to decay. Even as he stood there, it began to crack and give way. The castle was starting to crumble before his very eyes. Walls dripped with old, soaked wood. Windows shattered. Furniture was stripped of its fabric one thread at a time.

Frederick stood there, gripping his chest. *What is happening?* he wondered.

Of course, Frederick knew exactly what was happening.

He had eaten the egg.

He stumbled out of the house as quickly as he could and fell to the ground. Freddie sat and cried. The dreadful, dark growing pain of his stomach was no match for the pain of his heart. The pain of knowing what he had selfishly done for himself, in spite of the true happiness Tug had given him.

Freddie had convinced himself that Tug had left in disappointment, but as tears streamed down his face, he felt a soft furry hand reach out and wipe them away. They absorbed into Tug's fur. "Frederick, I'm here," Tug said as he joined Frederick on the ground.

Freddie looked right into Tug's yellow eyes. "Tug, what have I done?"

Tug began to cry and wrapped his arms around Frederick. "Everything will begin to fall apart. The grass will wither, the earth will crumble, and the sickness deep within your body will take your life away."

"How can I stop it?" Freddie cried in distress.

you cant but I CAN

Tug picked up Frederick and carried him to the river.

Freddie had gone to the river hundreds upon hundreds of times, but this time was very different. He just stared up at the tall trees and watched the wind direct their every move. With every gust, more and more leaves would fall. Not merely the yellow ones, but the green ones as well. This was followed by the limbs themselves, deteriorating in unison. All that was left to see in the sky were the stars, and then they, too, shuddered and became no more.

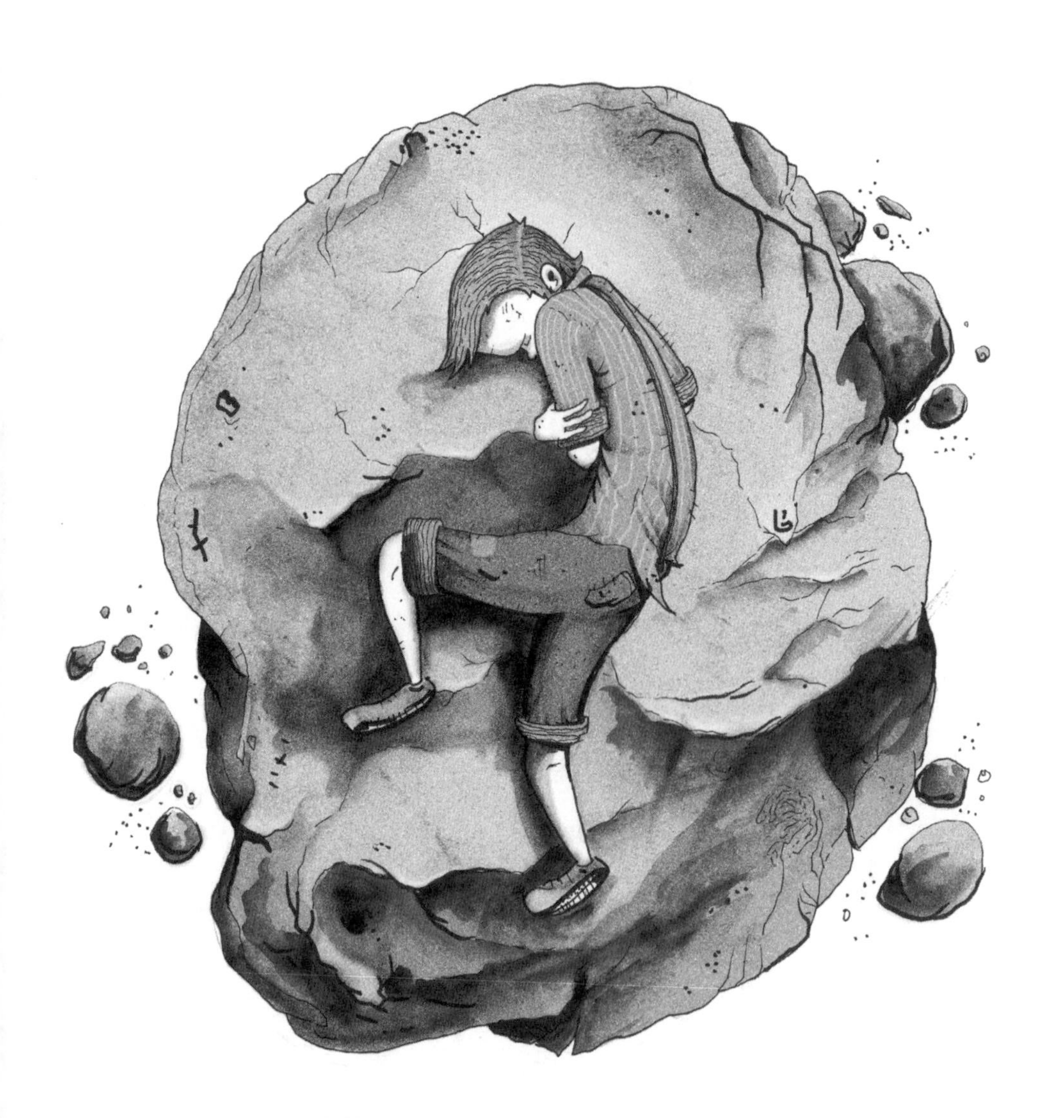

Gazing up at the empty black above, Frederick fully realized what he had done.

He gripped Tug that much tighter.

Tug didn't say a word. He just walked.

He stopped before a huge boulder and gently laid Frederick down.

"I love you, Frederick Cottonmouth," Tug said.

Freddie could no longer speak. The pain was too severe.

Tug walked toward the river. Freddie had dipped his toe in a time or two, but never his whole body. The river raged more heavily than after even the angriest of storms.

Tug forged ahead, water exploding around him with each step. He went deeper, until only his face and chest stood above the unrelenting current. He withstood the force as long as a beast of his enormous size could, then turned around and looked right into Frederick's eyes.

"It is finished," he said. Without another word, the water overtook him and he disappeared downstream.

Frederick's only response to Tug's death was tears. He could only cry himself to sleep. He slept for what felt like days on that boulder and only woke when the wing of a monarch butterfly grazed his cheek as it fluttered past. He sat up and stared hard at the water before him. He then climbed off the rock and picked a long blade of grass. He stuck it in his mouth and began to walk home. All the pain from eating the black egg was gone.

In fact, everything seemed normal. The grasshoppers were hopping. The clouds were in the same place as they always were. The yellow leaves … yellow.

Frederick walked back to where the mansion had once stood. In its place was the old Cottonmouth residence. There was no trace of what used to be. He stepped inside. Empty as before.

Frederick went to the closet under the stairs. Waiting for him was his fishing pole and the empty glass jar.

But before he reached them, there came a loud *CRACK* from upstairs.

Frederick stopped.

Looked up.

And smiled.